69329822R00111

Made in the USA
Columbia, SC
15 August 2019